For Jack and Betty, and my sisters who shared my peculiar pets - Vic xx

For Lola and Cordelia - love D

First published in 2009 by Alison Green Books
An imprint of Scholastic Children's Books
Euston House, 24 Eversholt Street
London NW1 1DB
A division of Scholastic Ltd
www.scholastic.co.uk
London ~ New York ~ Toronto ~ Sydney ~ Auckland
Mexico City ~ New Delhi ~ Hong Kong

Text copyright © 2009 Victoria Roberts
Illustrations copyright © 2009 Deborah Allwright

HB ISBN: 978 1 407104 35 5
PB ISBN: 978 1 407104 36 2
Printed in Singapore

1 3 5 7 9 10 8 6 4 2

The moral rights of Victoria Roberts and Deborah Allwright have been asserted.

Papers used by Scholastic Children's Books are made from wood grown in sustainable forests.

Victoria Roberts   Deborah Allwright

Peculiar Pets

ALISON
GREEN
BOOKS

Mum, can I have a pet?
Please?
Mum, Mum, can I?
Can I have a pet?

We'll see.

So I see . . .
I see a rock. A smooth rock.
I put string around it.

I call him **Fluffy**.

I take Fluffy for walks.

I let him off his lead
if he's good.

And he's good . . . for a day or two.

Mum, can I have a pet? **Please?**

Mum, Mum, can I?

Can I have a pet?

We'll see.

So I see . . .
I see a glove.
A soft woolly glove.

I put it in a basket.
I call her **Nibbles**.

I tickle Nibbles
in her basket.

I feed her
whenever she's hungry.

And she's hungry . . .

for a day or two.

Mum, can I have a pet?
Please?
Mum, Mum, can I?
Can I have a pet?

We'll see.

So I see . . .

I see a sweet wrapper.
A shiny sweet wrapper.

I put it in a bowl.
I call him William.

I give William water.
    I see him twist and turn as he swims.

And he swims . . .

for a day or two.

Mum, can I have a pet? **Please?**
Mum, Mum, can I?
Can I have a pet?

We'll see.

So I see . . .
I see a balloon.
A round balloon.

I draw a face on it.
I call him Bruce.

I stroke Bruce.

And he sticks to me
when we hug.

And we hug . . .

And we play . . .

And we dance about . . .
And Bruce is my best pet ever . . .

for a day or two.

N G!

Mum, Mum!
My pet popped!
He was my best pet ever
and now I can't play with him.

Oh, that's a pity.
Never mind.
Perhaps we can find another
pet for you to play with.

Let's see . . .

So we see . . .

We see a box.
A cardboard box.
We lift the lid.
We peep inside.

And we see . . .

Timmy the kitten!

And Timmy is the best pet
in the world!